To My Dear Friend - William,

Happy Birthday!
May you have a friend like
Puss in your life.
Love,
Nathan, Peter & MaryAnn

Copyright © 1999 by Nord–Süd Verlag AG, Gossau Zürich, Switzerland
First published in Switzerland under the title *Der gestiefelte Kater*
English translation copyright © 1999 by North-South Books Inc.

First published in the United States, Great Britain, Canada, Australia, and
New Zealand in 1999 by North-South Books, an imprint of Nord–Süd Verlag AG,
Gossau Zürich, Switzerland.

Distributed in the United States by North-South Books Inc., New York.

Library of Congress Cataloging-in-Publication Data is available.
A CIP catalogue record for this book is available from The British Library.

ISBN 0-7358-1158-X (trade binding)
1 3 5 7 9 TB 10 8 6 4 2
ISBN 0-7358-1159-8 (library binding)
1 3 5 7 9 LB 10 8 6 4 2

Printed in Belgium

For more information about our books, and the authors and artists who create
them, visit our web site: http://www.northsouth.com

# Charles Perrault
# PUSS IN BOOTS

ILLUSTRATED BY
## Giuliano Lunelli

Translated by Anthea Bell

## North-South Books
New York · London

Once upon a time there was a miller who had three sons, a mill, a donkey, and a clever, resourceful cat.

The donkey carried sheaves of wheat to the mill, the cat caught mice in the grain, and the miller's sons ground the flour.

When the miller died, he was so poor that there was no need for a lawyer to help his sons divide up his few possessions. The eldest son inherited the mill, the second son inherited the donkey, and nothing was left for the youngest but the cat.

"A cat!" said the youngest son, who was not very pleased with his share. "It's all very well for my brothers! If they work together they can still earn an honest living, but what am I to do with a cat?"

The cat had heard what the young man said. He washed his whiskers, and then spoke to his master in calm and sensible tones.

"Don't worry, master! You just listen to me. Get me a good pair of boots so that I can go out and about in company, and you'll soon find that your inheritance is not as bad as you think."

The miller's son was surprised to hear the cat talking, and he could not imagine what Puss was planning to do, but there was a cobbler living in the little town nearby, so he had the cat measured for a pair of boots.

When the cat had put on his fine new boots, he filled a bag with some carrots and fresh cabbage, slung it over his shoulder, and walked away on two legs, proud as a peacock.

After a while he came to a valley where a great many rabbits were running around. The cat hid behind a tree and waited.

Sure enough, a greedy young rabbit who knew nothing about the wicked ways of the world soon came along, tempted by the smell of the cabbage and hoping for a good meal. However, Master Cat pulled the strings of the bag tight, trapping the rabbit inside, and killed his catch.

Very proud of his success as a hunter, he went straight to the King's palace.

The palace guards were surprised to see a cat wearing boots—a talking cat, at that! "This cat will amuse His Majesty," said the guards, and they let him in.

So Puss strode into His Majesty's private rooms, bowed very low, and said, "Sire, my master, the Marquis of Carabas, has sent Your Majesty this excellent rabbit in his name, as a token of his loyalty and respect."

"Give your master my thanks," said the King graciously.

After that the cat went hunting every day, and he always took his catch to the palace and gave it to the King in the name of his master, the Marquis of Carabas. Before long he was as well known at court as if he were one of the King's closest friends.

One day he heard the coachman saying, "Oh, what a nuisance! I was going to play dice at the inn today, and now His Majesty insists on being taken for a drive!"

The cat soon discovered that the King was planning to drive along the banks of the river with his daughter, who was the most beautiful princess in the world. On learning this, Puss ran home to the miller's son as fast as he could go, and told him what he had heard.

"Take my advice, and your fortune is made," said the cat. "Go and swim in the river at a certain place—I'll show you where—and leave the rest to me."

The miller's son did as the cat said, although he had no idea what good it could possibly do him. When the King's coach drove up, the cat ran over to it, wailing most pitifully. "Oh, Your Majesty, my master was swimming in the river when some robbers came and stole all his clothes. Now he has nothing to wear, and can't get out of the water."

Seeing the Marquis of Carabas's servant, the King told his chamberlain to go back to the palace at once and fetch one of his own royal suits of clothes, the finest that could be found.

Meanwhile, the King's guards helped the miller's son out of the river, and the King spoke to him very kindly and graciously.

The fine clothes were a perfect fit for the miller's son, and since he was a handsome young man, the Princess was glad when the King invited him to join them on their drive.

Meanwhile Puss, delighted at the success of yet another clever trick, ran on ahead.

Soon he came to a large meadow that belonged to a powerful magician. "Good people," said Puss to the haymakers mowing the meadow, "in a moment the King will drive by, and if you don't tell him that this meadow belongs to the Marquis of Carabas, you'll all be made into mincemeat."

The haymakers were terrified, and when the King drove up and stopped to ask who owned the meadow, they all assured him, "It belongs to the Marquis of Carabas, Your Majesty."

"Well, you certainly own a beautiful meadow, Marquis," said the King to the miller's son. But the young man couldn't take his eyes off the lovely Princess sitting opposite him, and all he could stammer out was, "Oh yes, beautiful, beautiful, Your Majesty."

The cat ran on ahead of the coach again, and came to a large field where some reapers were cutting wheat.

"Good people," said the cat, "in a moment the King will drive by, and if you don't tell him that this field belongs to the Marquis of Carabas, every single one of you will be made into mincemeat."

Well, the reapers did not want to be made into
minccmcat, so whcn the King drove up and stopped
to ask who owned the field of wheat, they told him,
"It belongs to the Marquis of Carabas, Your Majesty."

The King was impressed, and paid the Marquis yet
more compliments on his great estates.

Soon after that the coach drove into a forest, where
some woodcutters were felling oaks and chopping them
up for timber. When the King asked the woodcutters
who owned the forest, they said, "Our master, the
Marquis of Carabas, Your Majesty." For of course the cat
had been there before the coach arrived, and had
warned the woodcutters, who were terrified of being
made into mincemeat.

The King was more impressed than ever.

At last the cat came to a magnificent castle. Like the
hay meadow, the wheat field, and the forest, it really
belonged to a great magician. The cat asked permission
to speak to him, saying he happened to be passing,
and couldn't possibly go on his way without paying his
deepest respects to so famous a master of magic.

The magician was flattered, and told his servants
to show Puss in.

"People say," said the cat, "that you can turn
yourself into any kind of animal you want, even an
elephant or a lion, but I really can't believe that!"

"Oh, you can't?" said the magician. "Just watch this!"
And in an instant he turned himself into a fierce,
roaring lion.

The terrified cat scurried right up to the ceiling,
although it was difficult to climb so high in his boots.

He didn't come down again until the magician had turned back into his usual shape.

"I've never seen anything like that before!" said Puss. "You most certainly are a master of your art. Very well, I admit you can turn into a lion, but I've also heard that if you want to, you can turn into a really tiny creature, like a rat or a mouse. However, that must surely be impossible!"

"Impossible?" said the magician with a smile, and to satisfy his visitor's curiosity he immediately turned himself into a little mouse running around the floor.

The cunning cat took one great leap—and that was the end of the mouse and the magician.

"However powerful you are, it's as well to be cautious!" said the clever cat, pleased with himself.

Just then the King came driving into the castle courtyard. Puss came out and opened the door of the coach with a deep bow.

"Welcome to my master's castle, Your Majesty! He is very happy indeed to receive you."

"Why, does this castle belong to you as well, Marquis?" cried the King. "I never saw anything finer in my life!"

The cat led them all into a magnificent banqueting hall, where a delicious meal was ready and waiting. Now that the King had seen what wealth and great estates the Marquis of Carabas owned, it struck him that the Marquis and the Princess made a handsome couple.

Raising his goblet, he said, "Marquis, if you'd care to be my son-in-law, I would have no objection at all!"

And the wedding was celebrated on the evening of the very same day.

As for Puss, who had arranged everything so cleverly, he was made Prime Minister and became a great lord.

However, he was strictly forbidden to tell any lies or make up any more stories, and so (like all Ministers of State) he never told anything but the truth.

And he never had to chase mice again, except for fun.